CALICO ILLUSTRATED CLASSICS

Daniel Defoe's

The Adventures of Robinson Crusoe

ADAPTED BY: Jan Fields

ILLUSTRATED BY: Eric Scott Fisher

magic wagon

visit us at www.abdopublishing.com

Published by Magic Wagon, a division of the ABDO Group,
8000 West 78th Street, Edina, Minnesota 55439. Copyright
© 2010 by Abdo Consulting Group, Inc. International copyrights
reserved in all countries. All rights reserved. No part of this book
may be reproduced in any form without written permission from
the publisher.

Calico Chapter Books™ is a trademark and logo of Magic Wagon.

Printed in the United States of America, Melrose Park, Illinois.
102009
012010

Original text by Daniel Defoe
Adapted by Jan Fields
Illustrated by Eric Scott Fisher
Edited by Stephanie Hedlund and Rochelle Baltzer
Cover and interior design by Abbey Fitzgerald

Library of Congress Cataloging-in-Publication Data

Fields, Jan.
  The adventures of Robinson Crusoe / adapted by Jan Fields ;
illustrated by Eric Scott Fisher ; based upon the work of Daniel
Defoe.
     p. cm. -- (Calico illustrated classics)
  ISBN 978-1-60270-703-0
  [1. Shipwrecks--Fiction. 2. Survival--Fiction. 3. Adventure and
adventurers--Fiction.] I. Fisher, Eric Scott, ill. II. Defoe, Daniel,
1661?-1731. Adventures of Robinson Crusoe. III. Title.
  PZ7.F479177Ad 2010
  [Fic]--dc22
                                               2009036526

Table of Contents

Out to Sea

My name is Robinson Crusoe. I was born in 1632 in the city of York. Being the third son of the family, I had no great hope of inheritance. My father planned for me to study law. I wanted to go to sea.

"Don't be foolish," Father scolded when I brought up the subject. "The sea is for the very wealthy or the very poor. The poor need to find fortune. The wealthy seek fame. But your life will be comfortable and steady."

Comfortable and steady seemed much like gloomy and dull to me. "I believe I can find greater happiness in adventure," I suggested.

At this my father's eyes filled with tears. "Do you not remember your brother? He craved a life of adventure and went to war. Where is he now? Would you go the same way?"

How could I press my case against such concern? I put all thoughts of the sea out of my mind for several weeks. But I could not settle down.

I finally spoke to my mother, hoping she might convince Father of my case. "Perhaps a short voyage," I suggested. "If it turns to misery as Father predicts, I will come home."

"How could you think such a thing?" Mother demanded. "After the talk you had with your father, we hoped such foolishness would have left you!"

Clearly I had only one option. I ran away. Not immediately, of course. I moped and complained for nearly a year. Then a friend suggested I travel with him by sea to London. Without a word to my parents, I boarded the boat.

On September 1, 1651, we set sail for London. Soon the wind blew heavily, driving waves against us. The ship leaped and bucked like an angry horse. My stomach leaped with it and I was most miserably sick.

I fell to my knees in my cabin and prayed that I would not die for disobeying my parents. Throughout the storm I bargained, begged, and promised. I would take up the law. I would be a good and obedient son.

Then the sea calmed. My stomach settled. The smooth sea with the sun upon it delighted me. And while I gazed upon the sea, my friend walked up and clapped me on the back.

"Did that capful of wind frighten you?" he asked.

"A capful!" I cried. "It was a terrible storm."

"That squall was nothing," he laughed. He must have noticed my doubtful face because he added with a grin, "Well, 'tis charming weather now. Let's settle down and celebrate your survival."

And so we did. In the merriment I forgot my vows. I forgot the storm. In the next five

or six days of good weather, I committed myself completely to the sea. I was certain that I would never regret my choice.

A few days later, the sky darkened. The wind blew hard. I laughed in the face of the storm. All hands gathered on deck to make everything snug as we rode the rough seas.

My stomach began to answer the roll of the sea. I retired to my cabin, sure I would soon see clear skies again. Then I heard the ship's master passing by my cabin door. "Have mercy on us," he prayed. "Let us not be lost!"

That begging did not ride well on my mind or my stomach. I got up and stumbled out of my cabin. The sea rose and broke upon us every few minutes. We cut away our masts so that the wind might not push us over.

A voice cried out, "All hands to the pumps!"

The ship had sprung a leak. Though fear made me clumsy, I followed the rest of the men and joined my strength to theirs.

Suddenly, a great boom rocked the ship. I knew the storm had broken the ship in two! I collapsed in a heap on the floor. A man stepped calmly over my body and took my place at the pump.

Another boom rang out. "What is it?" I screamed.

"The ship's gun," someone called. "The captain is signaling for help."

Finally, the captain's shots of distress were answered. A lighter craft risked the dangerous sea to bring the crew safely to port. Barely after leaving the ship, we watched it sink.

Rowing to shore took the strength of every man, but we made it. Do you imagine I rushed home the moment my feet touched shore? I pictured the knowing nods of my parents. I could not bear to be the butt of jokes about my foolish choices.

CHAPTER 2

Pirates!

My decision to return to the sea was sealed when I came upon my friend and his father one day. My friend introduced us and shared the story of how I came to sea.

"Young man," said the father, "you ought never to go to sea anymore. You are not meant to be a seafaring man."

The man sounded entirely too much like my father for my liking. I felt my backbone stiffen and my chin rise.

"You have seen the same token," I said. "Will you quit the sea?"

"My case is different," he replied. "The sea is my calling."

"I believe it is mine as well," I insisted. "I'll not turn away from it, no matter the predictions of you or my father."

"Then you make a choice that endangers anyone fool enough to sail with you," he said, backing away. "I would not set my foot in the same ship with you for a thousand pounds."

I was now determined to sail. I searched for another voyage that might appeal to me. I met the master of a ship that had recently come from Africa and was preparing to return.

The master was honest and kind. He took a liking to me, and we talked at length about my desire to see the world.

"You may ship with me," he said. "I'll show you the world and the fortunes a young man of courage can make."

I agreed and followed his directions perfectly. I turned to relatives to collect forty pounds to buy trinkets and toys. These I took aboard when we sailed.

The sail was smooth to the coast of Africa. The master spent many hours teaching me about navigation, record keeping, and other such bits of seaman's craft. I soaked up his knowledge like a sponge, and we grew as close as family.

Not only did the voyage educate me, but it enriched me as well. I returned to London with five pounds of gold dust. I had settled upon my life's calling. I would be a merchant and sail with my friend, growing richer with each trip.

The ship's master took me home with him. I met his fine wife and we made plans for the next sail. Unfortunately, before our plans could come to be, the kind man died.

I left the bulk of my earnings with his widow in safekeeping and shipped out again as a merchant. It was the same ship, but sadly not the same master. And with the loss of my good friend, my luck seemed to slip away as well.

Near the northern African shore, we were set upon by a Turkish pirate ship. We tried to outrun the pirates, but they had the faster ship. We fired upon them with our twelve small cannons and they returned fire with their eighteen cannons and smaller guns as well.

The pirate ship sailed close and sixty men jumped over to board us. We fought back. We even tossed powder chests, which exploded and scattered deadly bits of nails and scrap iron.

The pirates hacked at our rigging. They killed three of our bravest men and wounded more. Finally, we surrendered and were taken aboard their ship as prisoners.

We were carried to the pirate base at Sallee. Then, the captives were taken to be presented to the Moorish emperor. I alone stayed, as the pirate captain's prize. And so I began my life as a slave.

A Clever Escape

I plotted to escape. I hoped I might sail with the pirates and be freed when an English ship took them captive. But whenever the pirates sailed, I was left behind.

Over the next two years, my position in the house slowly rose. The captain learned I was good at fishing. He took me with him on trips in a small fishing boat whenever he was home.

Eventually, he began letting me fish with only his cousin Ismael and a young slave named Xury. Though Ismael served as guard on these trips, he was young and paid little attention. He treated me as a coworker instead of a slave.

One day, the captain planned a fishing and bird-hunting trip with some local men. The boat was filled with food and guns. At the last moment, the men decided they would remain at the master's house. I was sent to catch fish for their supper.

Surely, I thought, *no greater opportunity will come my way.* I fished for some time but made certain to catch nothing, urging Ismael to go farther and farther to catch the fish the master would want.

Finally, I was content we had gone as far as we dared. I crept up behind Ismael and tossed him into the water.

He rose immediately, coughing. "Wait!" he called. "Don't leave me here to drown with the sharks!"

At first I ignored him, but he swam strongly toward the boat. I had no choice but to take up a gun.

"You swim well," I called to him. "You'll have no trouble reaching shore. But if you come nearer this boat, I'll shoot you."

Ismael turned quickly away from the boat and swam for shore. Then I turned to Xury and said, "If you'll remain faithful to me, I'll make you a great man."

I nodded pointedly at the gun. "But if you'll not swear to be true to me, I'll throw you in the sea as well."

The young boy smiled at me and eagerly promised his faithfulness. We struck out to sea with the boat. I was terrified the pirates would catch us again, so we sailed without stopping for five days.

Finally, the need for fresh water pushed me toward land. We found the water we needed but quickly hurried back to our boat. On our stops, I depended on Xury to spot game, skin animals, and such. He depended upon me for the protection of the guns.

We saw no sign of people for many days, but finally we passed a shore upon which a small group stood. They wore few clothes and their

skin was very dark. We did not go ashore, and they showed no interest in coming closer.

I made gestures to them that we were hungry and thirsty. Several dashed away and returned with meat and dried vegetables. A great clay container filled with water was carried to the shore.

Suddenly, two great cats burst from the thick trees not far from the beach. Most of the people ran in fear, but one man stayed. He held a long stick and seemed intent on protecting the group.

As soon as the cats appeared, Xury fetched my guns. I shot the larger of the two cats and the other ran way from the sound of the gun.

I made signs that I wanted the people to have the cat. They were clearly delighted. They skinned it with nothing more than a knife made of wood, and offered me the skin. I accepted it gladly.

We parted company with each side content. Xury and I sailed for eleven more days until the shore began to point slightly out to sea. In the distance, I could make out islands. I was certain we had come upon the Cape de Verde.

Suddenly Xury called out, "Master, a ship with a sail!"

I could hear the fear in his voice and knew he worried that the ship contained more pirates. I recognized the vessel as a Portuguese ship.

I sailed fast toward it and fired the guns, hoping the sound would catch their attention. I waved the flag that had belonged to the past captain, desperate to catch the eye of the Portuguese seamen.

The ship allowed us to approach. The sailors called out to me, first in Portuguese, then Spanish and French. I understood none of these and called back in English.

At last a Scotch sailor was found to be my translator. I was able to tell them of my escape from slavery. I was so grateful for rescue that I offered all I had to the captain in thanks.

"You owe me nothing," the captain assured me. "I have offered only what I would hope to receive in your place. We will carry you safely to the Brazils. You will need your things to make your way there."

He commanded his crew that none should touch my things. He bought the small boat I had sailed on and the animal skins I had collected.

"I would like to buy the boy also," he said, gesturing to Xury.

"He helped me escape," I said. "I should not sell him back into slavery."

"Then let me not buy his whole life," the captain said. "Let me buy ten years of his service aboard the ship, after which he shall go free."

I turned to Xury to see what he would say. I did not wish to insult the captain, but I owed Xury much. Xury agreed that he would sail with the captain for ten years and the bargain was struck.

Shipwrecked

We had a good sail to the Brazils and arrived in about twenty-two days. I carried a small bag of silver coins and all the belongings that the captain had not bought.

I lived for a while on a sugar plantation run by a friend of the captain. I learned the basics of growing and making sugar. It seemed a good life and profitable. I bought as much land as I could and began planting.

I sent to England for the money I had left with my friend's widow. With it, I was able to buy a slave and an indentured servant to help with the work.

But life as a plantation owner grew dull. I wanted to be on the sea again. So I made a plan.

Every plantation needed more workers than we could hire. I went to the owners with a proposal. If they would fund the voyage, I would set sail for Africa and purchase slaves. Then I would distribute them to the various plantations.

This idea met with approval. On September 1, 1659, I boarded our ship for Africa. I scarcely noted that this was the same date I had boarded my first ship eight years before!

We sailed well northward before striking out across the ocean toward Africa. The weather was good, though brutally hot until we turned out to sea.

Some twelve days later, a fierce storm slammed our ship for a dozen days, driving us wherever it would. At every moment, I expected to die. Indeed, two of the crew were washed overboard by the storm.

Finally, the storm died back and the captain looked for a place to bring the ship ashore. The ship was too damaged to attempt a sea crossing now. The captain decided to press north to Barbados, which looked reachable. But only a few days later another storm struck and pushed us westward.

"Land!" the watchman shouted from the rigging. He pointed into the roaring storm. "Land!"

We rushed to see. Suddenly, the ship struck upon a sandbar and stopped. The sea washed over the sides as if to cleanse the broken ship.

The ship had carried two small boats. One had been smashed in the storm. We needed to launch the last boat and row away from the broken ship if we were to survive the day.

The mate laid hold of the boat and we helped sling it over the ship's side. Eleven of us piled in. We had no sails, only oars.

The winds fell, but the sea rose violently as we struggled toward land. A massive wave turned us and we were scattered into the sea.

The raging waves tossed me. My lungs burned as I rolled and tumbled under the water. Then a wave scooped me up and carried me so close to shore that I could stand.

I scrambled for dry land, but another wave scooped me up. I struggled to stay above water. This wave carried me still closer to shore.

Each time a wave dropped me, I found my feet and staggered forward, trying helplessly to outrun the next rush.

The waves would deliver me to land eventually, but I had no great hope of being alive as they battered me all the way. Finally a wave dashed me against a rock, leaving me senseless.

When I recovered, I saw the force of the waves had calmed. I clung to the rock until I felt strong enough to make a last run for land. At the retreat of another wave, I clambered up the cliffs to sit upon the grass. I had survived.

I walked the shore, searching for signs of other survivors. I did not spot even a hat or a

shoe. I could make out the wreck of our ship in the far distance. How had I survived?

I had no food, no water—not even dry clothes. I went through my pockets and found a knife, a tobacco pipe, and a small tin of tobacco. My chances for survival seemed slight indeed.

CHAPTER
5

The Island

I headed away from shore and was delighted to find a clear spring. Then I cut myself a stout stick to use as a weapon and climbed a tree. There I slept the first night in my new home.

The morning dawned clear. I felt surprisingly refreshed after a night in a tree. I headed back to shore, where I discovered that the storm had driven the broken ship from the sandbar. The waves had set it on the rocks within a mile of shore.

I also found the boat that we had struck out in. A fast-flowing inlet lay between me and the boat. I decided to deal with the broken ship first as it held more useful items.

The tide crept out farther and farther until I could walk upon sand to within a quarter mile of the ship. I realized all of us would have survived the storm if we'd only stayed with the ship.

I cried at the thought of how easily I could be sharing this adventure with a group. But this was no time for tears. I wiped my face and slipped out of my clothes so I could swim to the ship.

Once I reached it, I swam around looking for a way to get aboard. I spotted a hanging bit of rope and used it to climb the side.

I found the ship's food was free of water. I filled my mouth with biscuits. Now I only needed a boat to get the food to shore.

I collected boards and bits of sail. I tied the sails together before tossing them overboard. Then I lashed the boards together into a raft. I laid more planks across my raft so that anything I put on it would be safe from the water.

Next, I found three seamen's chests. I filled them with bread, rice, cheese, dried goat meat, and a small bag of chicken feed.

After I had filled my raft, I looked toward shore. I discovered the tide was coming in and had washed my clothes away! I was forced to add a set of clothes to my rummaging.

Finally I added guns, ammunition, and some tools to my growing pile. When I dared add no more weight, I collected some oars and headed for land.

A current swept me well past the spot I had landed before. I spotted an inlet and struck out for it. The sea flowed naturally toward it, and it was easy enough to slip in.

After I had washed upstream a bit in the inlet, I used my oars to land the raft in a shallow area. I then waited for the tide to go out and the water to lower me onto the dry land. When it did, I easily unloaded my cargo.

My spirits were as high as any could hope for. I decided to hike to the tallest point I could find and learn what I could about my situation. I carried a pistol, powder, and shot with me and hiked up a small mountain.

From the top, I saw that I was truly the lone human on the island. There were two smaller islands a distance away. I saw no sign of large animals, but I did see birds.

That night I built a kind of hut. I used the chests and boxes I carried from the ship. When all was done, I slept on the ground.

CHAPTER
6

A Proper Settlement

I decided to make a daily trip to the ship for as long as I was able. I knew a single storm could push the wreck beyond my reach.

On my second trip to the ship, I worried about leaving my food behind. It was locked in a sea chest, but that might not keep large beasts away.

My worry was for nothing as the only creature I saw after any of my trips was a small cat. As I approached, it ran away a little distance then stopped to stare at me.

"What do you want?" I asked, thinking the cat might flee at the sound of my voice. But it only stared at me.

I raised my gun toward it but still it looked into my face with no sign of fear. As this was the friendliest face I had seen since the wreck, I broke off a bit of biscuit and tossed it.

The cat walked to it, sniffed it, then ate it daintily. It looked up at me again as if to ask for more.

"Thank you for your welcome," I said politely. "But I cannot spare more biscuit." And so it marched off, ending my first encounter with the island's native population.

While carrying all the ship's goods to land, I found two cats and a dog locked in a cabin. I brought them to shore. The cats thanked me by stalking off into the jungle.

The dog stayed by my side for many years. I had only to point at something and he would fetch it. He did all that he could for me. But the thing I wanted most, he could not do. He could not speak to me, though I spoke often to him.

As my collection of goods grew each day, I was able to build a more impressive shelter. I made a little tent with a piece of sail and some poles. I brought everything that might spoil into the tent.

Around the tent I piled all the empty chests to protect the canvas. I made a kind of door with boards inside the tent and an empty chest on the outside. With a more solid shelter, I slept soundly each night. I faced each morning fresh for another search of the ship.

I found enough ammunition to keep me well armed. I also carried away more tools, scrap metal, rope, sails, a hammock, bedding, and even silverware!

On my twelfth trip, I came upon money. "What good art thou to me?" I asked the coins. At first, I thought to leave them, but I finally bundled them up and carried them away.

On my way back from this trip, the wind picked up and the sea grew rougher. I was grateful when my feet touched ground again.

I hurried home to my little tent, where I lay secure with all my wealth about me. The wind blew hard all night. In the morning, the ship was gone from the rocks. It now lay well beyond my reach, but I was confident I had all I needed from it.

After I had been ashore a dozen days, I realized how difficult it became to keep track of the days. So I cut a large post and carved into it with my knife: "I came on Shore here on the 30th of Sept. 1659."

Each day that passed, I cut a notch. For every seventh day, I cut a longer notch. Then at the start of each new month, I cut the longest notch of all. Thus I could keep track of the days, weeks, and months far more easily.

I cried many a tear from loneliness and self-pity. But, it helped that I was busy creating a proper settlement for myself. I needed a place where I could be secure and where I could watch for passing ships.

I soon found a safe place on the side of a hill. I set about building a fence from long stakes. At over five feet tall, this fence would not be easily scaled by wild beasts or humans. I made no door to my fence. Instead, I used a rope ladder that could be pulled inside.

I brought all my riches inside the fence. Then, I set about creating a large tent with a smaller tent inside. This kept me secure against the violent rains that fell at certain times of year.

I hung the hammock I had retrieved from the ship. It was a comfortable bed each night. I made a table and chair from the short pieces of board I had rescued from the ship.

I was a very sorry workman, having never built anything before. But I learned much from the process. I remade the chair several times before I was happy with it.

Putting Things in Order

Now that I had a secure home and a place to sit, I began my journal. In the first entries, I recorded most of what I have shared here.

My days were divided into two sections. I hunted in the mornings then napped when the day grew too hot for movement. When the day cooled, I worked around my homestead.

My living space was tightly packed with belongings. I decided to dig a pantry into the hill behind my tent.

It was mid-November before I could really work hard at my pantry. I suffered for the lack of pickax, shovel, or wheelbarrow.

My need for a shovel was pressing, so I searched for items to make the tool. I found what I believed to be an Iron Tree, named for its weight and hardness. With difficulty I managed to collect a piece and haul it home.

Working the wood into a rough spade shape was long and hard. Though the end result looked odd, I was satisfied that no shovel ever had more work in the making.

As I dug out my pantry, I used the dirt to level and raise the land all around my tent. Over time, my cave storage area grew bigger and bigger and my home became tidy.

By early December, I was convinced my cave was big enough for all my goods. In fact, I had dug out too much. Part of the roof and side caved in, which alarmed me more than a bit!

Digging the rubble out of my cave was no small task. Then I learned to cut trees and create the shoring for the storeroom. This shoring strengthened the walls and allowed me to add long wooden shelves. I found great pleasure at seeing my things so neatly in order.

With the pantry finished, I looked around for what to do next. Near the end of December, I lamed a young goat on a hunting expedition. I caught it and led it home on a string.

When I had the goat home, I bound up its leg and took care of it. It grew tame and never wandered far away.

At this, I considered the potential in taming and breeding goats. I hunted for a mate for my goat. But when I brought the dog to the herd, they didn't scatter so that he might cut one from the group. Instead, they turned and faced him. The dog sensed his danger and would go no farther.

Since I seemed unable to catch more than one goat, I turned my attention to my storage rooms. I took inventory of what I owned and planned ways to make anything I was missing. During my search, I learned that rats had gotten into the bag of chicken feed and eaten the contents. I decided to use the empty bag to hold powder for my gun.

I shook the dusty remains out of it on the ground outside the cave and gave it no further thought. A month or so later, I noticed a few green stalks shooting up out of the ground. I watched the plant grow, wondering what it might be. I was astonished when it bore perfect green English barley!

If this was not enough of a surprise, I found some stalks of rice nearby. I realized that what I had thought was a dusty bag of spoiled feed had become a farm. I saved the grain carefully that I might plant it again and increase my harvest over time.

CHAPTER 8

Exploring the Island

By April, I thought myself quite set indeed. My home was neat and I even had an accidental farm. Then, one day as I was in my storage area, I felt a rumbling shiver in the ground. Dirt and rubble rained down on my head. One of my beams cracked. My cave was falling in again!

I raced out of my pantry, panting from fear. Then I felt the rumble again. The trembling was not caused by a cave-in. An earthquake was shaking the island!

Suddenly, a huge rock about half a mile from me split in two. A great piece tumbled down the mountain. My fear grew to panic. Rock could fall on me at any moment. It could crush my home and everything I had.

The rumbling finally stopped, but still I sat on the ground. I was too frightened to return to my home.

As I sat, the sky grew cloudy and the wind picked up until a hurricane roared through. Trees crashed to the ground. For three hours, the wind roared across the island. Then the rain fell.

The rain drove me back to my cave. It rained all night and much of the next day. As I waited out the rain, I knew I must move my home. A tent and cave set under a rock overhang was the most dangerous choice I could have made. I decided I would build a hut well away from falling rock.

When the rain finally stopped, I looked around my home. I was struck again by how much I liked it and how proud I was of the work I had done. I did not want to leave it and start again. So I kept my home but considered a plan for a second lodging.

As I checked the beach after the storm, I discovered that it had driven the wreck of my ship back to shore! It was so close I could walk out to it easily. I decided to dismantle the ship and save as much as I possibly could.

Each morning in May and well into June, I walked to the wreck and retrieved as much as I could before the tides came in. One day, I found a turtle on the shore. It made a nice change to my diet of goat and pigeon.

This meal was the last pleasant time for weeks as I came down with a terrible fever. My head ached and I seemed to rock between being icy cold and sweaty with fever. Too weak to get out of bed, I eventually ran out of water. Soon, thirst added to my weakness and misery.

Though I did not die, I was weak for many days. After being so close to death, I turned to one of the Bibles I had rescued from the ship. I hoped to find a scripture to explain my life. None came, but I found refreshment in the reading just the same.

By mid-July, I was strong and set out to explore the entire island. I found a small valley with grapes that I dried into raisins. I found limes as well.

I was delighted with this little valley filled with fruit and good water. I built a small shelter there. I even considered moving, but I trusted the security of my hillside fortress.

My island did not have seasons like in Europe. Instead, the year was divided into times of great dryness and times of heavy rain. There were two of each in every year.

All of March and September were rainy, as well as half of February, August, and October. The other parts of the year were dry. This helped me plan my growing seasons and where I would live in each part of the year.

As the rainy season came, I headed to my stronghold with a good supply of dried grapes. There, I met the anniversary of my arrival on the island and spent the day in prayer and fasting.

During the dry season, I returned to my holiday home. I discovered that the stakes I had cut for my fence had sprouted and grown! I cut more stakes and hauled them back to my first fortress. I planted them on the outside of that thick wall. They grew there, too.

Soon both of my fences offered not only protection but invisibility. They seemed to blend into the jungle around them.

Near my holiday home, I began making baskets with the wood and vines there. My baskets helped much in hauling things around the island.

The more I explored the island, the more I saw my original homestead was on the most meager part. On my travels, I found areas of lush fruit and beaches covered with turtles.

One day, my dog ran upon a young goat. I brought it home to be tamed. My last tame goat had grown old and cranky, so I was glad to add to my tiny flock.

Thus I spent my second year on the island in exploration and small improvements. I found it pleasant overall and my fortress now felt very much like home to me.

Island Life

I missed human companionship, but I found exploring to be an exciting pastime. And I enjoyed the company of my creatures. I had captured and tamed a parrot to add to my household. He learned to say a number of things, and I delighted in the sound of a voice.

I also spent much time in prayer and reading the Bible. I found great comfort in the spiritual side of my life.

I finally had enough grain to plant in earnest. I built a wall around my garden to keep the wild goats away. Then when my crop bore its fruit, the birds discovered it.

The birds were not bothered at all by the fence or the barking dog. I shot amongst them and brought down several birds, but as soon as I walked away, they returned.

I hung bird corpses amongst the crop, hoping it would convince the other birds to stay away. These scarecrows were successful. By harvest time, I had nearly two bushels of rice and two and a half bushels of barley.

With my new grain to store, I found a new problem. The fine grain slipped through the cracks in my rough baskets. I decided to try my hand at pottery.

It took me nearly two months to find clay, dig it out, and form and dry oddly shaped, ugly pots. In the end, I had exactly two pots—one for rice and one for barley.

I also wanted vessels that could hold water. So I experimented with heating my pots to make them harder. After many broken and spoiled attempts, I finally came upon the right balance of heat and time.

Next I formed a clay oven and began baking bread. I had fashioned a mortar and pestle from hard wood, and I made a sifter from cloth. I made small loaves of barley bread and baked them in my oven. I spent the third year on the island in farming and baking.

Soon after that, I began to think of my days sailing in a tidy boat with Xury. I longed to explore the island by sea. I feared what I might find on the neighboring islands, but I could not shake the desire for a boat.

I tried to retrieve the ship's boat that I had seen washed up. The boat had been flipped over by wind or waves. I found I could not turn her right side up. I tried rollers, levers, and digging before giving up.

I was still determined to have a boat. I choose a strong cedar and spent weeks cutting it down and stripping it of limbs. Then I spent months transforming it from tree to canoe.

When it was time to launch, I realized I had made my canoe too far from the nearest stream. The boat was far too heavy for one man to

move. I tried bringing the water to the boat instead of the boat to the water. I soon saw that chore would take me twenty years of constant labor.

I celebrated my fourth year on the island with two boats, but I was no closer to a sea journey.

CHAPTER 10

The Sixth Year

With four years on the island, I ran out of ink to keep my journal. Also, my clothes hung in tatters. The weather was so hot I little needed clothes, but I could never quite bring myself to do without.

I had always saved the skins of the creatures I hunted, and I decided to use them for clothing. I was not a skilled tailor. The hat I made to keep off the sun and the rain made me glad of having no mirror to see myself.

I made a waistcoat and breeches open at the knees. I wore them loose that I might stay cool. I must have looked frightful in my hairy clothes, though neither dog nor parrot complained.

After this, I made myself an umbrella to keep heat and rain off. I had to make several before I hit upon a way to make it go up and down.

With clothes and protection from the sun, I turned again to boat making. I made a smaller boat and took care to build it close to a stream that led to the sea. I fitted up a little mast to my boat and made a sail out of the ship's sail I had kept.

I made little boxes for either end of the boat where I might store provisions. I cut a long hollow place inside the boat to rest my gun. Then, I fashioned a flap to cover it and keep it dry.

After several short voyages I decided it was time to sail round the island. I packed barley cakes, parched rice, and dried goat.

On November 6 of my sixth year on the island, I began my sail around it. It took longer than I expected, as rocky shoals required me to sail far from shore in several places.

At one point, I brought my boat close in. I anchored and climbed a hill to see the shoreline ahead. A fast current rushed beyond the rocky shoals. I feared I might find myself caught in the current and pushed out to sea, so I stayed on the shore.

On the third morning after setting anchor, the sea lay very calm. I decided to sail. Soon I found myself caught up in the current. Neither sail nor oar could control my craft. I was certain I would be driven into the sea and be lost.

I fought to get as close to the shore as I could manage. But with each passing moment the distance seemed to grow wider.

Finally the wind picked up and my sails filled. At the same time, a group of rocks seemed to split the current. I rode the half that pushed closer to the island.

When I finally gained the shore again, I fell on my knees and thanked God. I slept, having been exhausted by the trip. I struck out again the next day but hugged the shore tightly. I was determined not to be pushed to sea again.

Finally I spied a natural harbor where my boat could rest safely. I docked there and went ashore. I found myself on the part of the island nearest my small valley. So taking nothing from my boat but my gun and my umbrella, I hiked to my country home.

I barely made it inside before I collapsed in the shade to sleep. Hours later, I was wakened by a voice calling, "Robin, Robin, Robin Crusoe. Where are you? Where are you?"

I awoke in some fright to spy my parrot, Poll. The bird peered at me and flapped its wings before asking, "Where are you, Robin Crusoe?"

I could not imagine how Poll had gotten from my fortress home to my country home. But I was delighted to see him. He seemed overjoyed to see me as well.

The Mysterious Footprint

After the fright of my short voyage, I decided to give up sea travel. I spent a quiet year ashore. I turned my attention again to goats. I knew eventually my powder would run out and my gun would be no better than a club. I needed my own flock.

I tried snares to catch the goats. For most of my efforts, I did little more than feed the wild goats with my grain. But finally, I managed to capture several kids and a cranky old male.

Taming the male seemed impossible and any contact with him was dangerous. So, I pushed a log into the trap and he escaped.

The kids I tied with strings and led back to my summer home. I built a large enclosure with plenty of access to green grass and fresh water. I visited regularly, feeding the goats from my hand so that they were truly tame.

By the end of the year, I had begun my life as a dairy man. The tame goats provided meat and milk. I taught myself to make butter and cheese. I now had fruit, raisins, goat meat, turtle, fowl, butter, cheese, rice, and barley cakes.

I kept my dairy herd on the summer side of the island. My main home was on the other side of the island. I spent much time traveling back and forth.

I also checked on my boat often. I would take the boat out from shore for quick sails now and again. I had to be certain it remained sea worthy and to check for any repairs needed.

It was on one of these walks to check on my boat that I froze at an impossible sight. I found a single human footprint pressed into the sand. The foot was bare. The imprint was clear, it could be nothing but the step of a man.

I spun around, peering into the jungle. Then I fled as if the devil himself were chasing me. I imagined each tree became another native pursuing me. I cowered in my fortress home for several days, expecting an attack at any moment.

Finally, I calmed myself enough to give real thought to the footprint. Perhaps I was scaring myself over a print I had made myself. Surely the print was mine and no other. I laughed at my own foolishness and headed out to examine the print again.

When I reached it, I placed my own bare foot beside it. The print was larger than mine in all ways. This was not my foot.

Perhaps, I told myself, *a native from another island had been blown onto my island. In that case, he surely took his boat and left as quickly as possible. Certainly, he is no longer here.*

Still, I spent the next two years increasing the security around my home. I even set muskets into the walls so that I might hold off

a host of intruders if need be. I decided to divide my flock so that any visitor could not carry off my entire food supply.

I built another enclosure in a thickly wooded area of the island. Again I made sure there was food and water. I led ten young females and two young males into the enclosure and shut them up. Now I needed just one more enclosure.

I planned to set the third pen on the far western part of the island. I had never been there. It would give me the farthest placement for my third herd and also allow me to know the full reaches of my kingdom.

I climbed a hill overlooking the western shore and peered into the distance. I thought for a moment that I saw a boat, but it was too far to be certain. I had no glass with me. I had taken several from the ship but was not in the habit of carrying them.

I climbed down the hill to the beach. What I saw there choked me with fear and disgust.

The shore was spread with skulls and other bits of bone that could only come from human bodies.

Nearby, a scorched well revealed where someone had made a fire. Was this the remains of a feast where the main course was human?

So great was my shock, I turned away and vomited. Not only had my island been visited regularly, it had been the feasting ground for the worst kind of horror. I fled, running to my sturdy home.

Living in Fear

For the next several years, I kept close to my own homesteads, staying far from the western shore. Gradually I realized that I had lived eighteen years on the island with no contact with these people. I would surely never make contact!

Still, whenever I left my fortress I carried my gun and wore two pistols tucked in my goat-hide belt. I never fired them for fear of attracting attention.

Thus armed, I resumed my treks to tend the goats. Through all my work, my mind turned again and again to the horrifying visitors. Sometimes I thought of rescuing their victims.

Other times I plotted ways I might frighten the killers so they would leave my island forever.

Though the plots and plans kept my mind busy, I had to discard each one as being too dangerous. But the idea would not go away.

Finally I settled upon finding an uphill station where I might wait for boats to arrive on the island. My plan was to fire upon them before they could even exit to the beach.

After a few treks, I found myself questioning my plan. What right had I to shoot at men from a hiding place? Would that not be murder?

So I returned to my own life. I removed my little boat from the water and hid it. I decided that I would keep to myself.

I must admit, I never felt the ease that I had once known. I made note of everything I did and whether it might reveal me. I winced at the sound of a driving nail or the bite of the ax into wood.

My fires also worried me. How far might the smoke carry? Could I be discovered simply by cooking broth or firing my pottery? I decided that I must make some charcoal that would burn without the smoke of an open fire.

While scouting for trees to make into charcoal, I made another discovery. I found a hollow in a rock and crept into it. It was a cave. I could stand comfortably though the ceiling was low.

As I peered into the gloom, I was certain I saw the sparkle of eyes. I scrambled out in fear. Then, I snatched up a firebrand and rushed back into the cave.

Inside, I heard a very loud sigh of pain and then vague mutterings. The hairs crept up on my arms and the back of my neck.

I plucked up my courage and stepped deeper into the gloom. I found an elderly goat close to death. He had apparently wandered into the cave to die of old age. I edged around the poor beast and explored the rest of the cavern.

At the back, I found another small hole that led into a huge cavern. The ceiling must have been at least twenty-five feet above me. As I held my torch up, the light from it reflected off the walls. The cavern appeared to be walled with crystal all around.

I wasn't certain what to do with this discovery, but I soon set this cave up as another shelter on the island. It seemed wise to have

many places I could dart into and stay safe if need be.

I resolved to be less timid as I went about my island routine. If I avoided the west end of the island, surely I could spend another thirty years without ever seeing another human.

CHAPTER
13

A Guest

On a December morning of my twenty-third year on the island, I was surprised to see the light of fire upon the shore. My shore. On my side of the island.

I pulled the ladders into my castle and cowered inside. The wildness of my home blended perfectly with the jungle, but there was plenty that could give me away. My harvest fields alone revealed clear signs of man.

Finally, I had to know what was going on. I lay upon my stomach on the highest rock I could find. I used my spyglass to watch the group on the shore. I spotted nine men and watched them on and off until they left.

Now that I knew even my side of the island was not sacred, I worried constantly about attack. For the next year, I could barely sleep for fear of waking to a knife at my throat.

In the middle of the following year, a fierce storm struck. I heard the firing of a great gun. I listened and the sound came again. Surely, a ship was calling for help. I built a huge fire on the highest rock above my fortress and fed it throughout the stormy hours of night.

In the morning, I turned my glass out to sea and was certain I spied a ship. I watched it all that day. It never moved. It was either at anchor or stuck upon the rocks offshore.

I raced to the south shore of the island. There, I found that the ship was indeed stuck on the rocks.

I brought my own small boat out to the wreck, imagining the joy of rescuing a fellow castaway. But when I reached the ship, I found only a half-starved dog and two dead sailors.

I shared my food and water with the dog. Then, I searched the ship for goods I might carry away. I found three pairs of shoes. I also found a kettle, a small pot, and a number of good shirts.

I also collected some money, though that was the least useful thing of all. I was grateful for the dog, since my own had passed away in the eighteenth year of my stay. But I longed for human contact.

Not long after this, I had the most peculiar dream. In my dream, a boat carried a host of natives and two prisoners. One of the prisoners broke away and ran through the jungle to beat upon the walls of my fortress. I lowered down a ladder to bring him up to me. His captors searched for him, but could not see that my wild home was anything more than trees.

In my dream, the prisoner I saved became my servant and companion and I felt truly happy and content.

Another year and a half passed. Once again, I found canoes coming ashore on my side of the island. This time there were no less than five canoes. This meant twenty or thirty killers, and I dared not think I could win against such numbers.

Still, I crept closer. I saw two victims pulled from the canoes and dragged toward the fires. One of them was quickly clubbed as I watched in horror. While the focus of the group was on that man, the other victim ran.

His speed across the sand was amazing to see. He quickly outdistanced the men chasing him. I saw that he was running straight toward my fortress. This similarity to my dream was not lost on me.

Only three men chased the captive across the sand. Then the prisoner reached the wide creek that lay between the shore and my castle. I thought surely that he would be recaptured, but he threw himself into the water and swam strongly across.

The men chasing the captive reached the banks of the creek. One could not swim as he stayed on the beach side. The other two dived in and swam across.

I saw now that it was my calling to save this man's life. I rushed toward the men with my gun in my hands. I yelled to the running man, cutting between him and his pursuers. I knocked the first of his captors down with the butt of my gun.

The second man froze. I thought for a moment that he was frightened of me in my wild, hairy clothes. But he was fumbling for a bow and arrow. Seeing no other choice, I shot him.

I turned then toward the escaped man. He trembled in terror at the roar and smoke of my gun. I spoke to him quietly, hoping to show him I meant him no harm.

He crept closer to me, walking a few steps and stopping as if still considering running away instead. During these pauses he would kneel, perhaps to show me he meant no harm even as I was showing him the same.

Finally he reached me and knelt again. He kissed the ground. He laid his head on the ground, then lifted my foot and placed it on his head.

I was not certain what this gesture meant. He treated it like a ritual. Perhaps he was swearing some kind of loyalty to me. I helped him to his feet and with smiling and patting showed myself to be his friend.

At this moment, I realized that the native I had struck with my gun was not dead. He roused himself until he was sitting.

My new friend spoke, though the words meant nothing to me. Still, I enjoyed the sound of another human voice. He gestured to the sword I wore at my belt and I gave it to him. Then he rushed at the man and cut off his head in a single stroke.

I was stunned at first but could see why my new friend would have no love for his captors.

The young man walked over to the fallen native I had shot. He stared intently at the hole in the man's chest.

Finally he gathered the bow and arrows from the fallen man and headed back to me. He signed that we should bury the bodies in the sand. I agreed and he fell swiftly to digging.

He worked so quickly that it was obvious I would only be in the way. He buried the bodies in the space of no more than a half hour.

After this chore was done, I led my new friend to the cave I had found most recently. I was not completely ready to bring him to my fortress. Still, in many ways, my dream had come true. I was no longer alone in my kingdom.

Teaching Friday

I gave the young man I had rescued bread, raisins, and water. After his run, burying his pursuers, and hiking to the cave, he was exhausted. I showed him a pallet and blanket and he fell quickly asleep.

As I studied him, I guessed his age at around twenty-six. He was tall with straight, strong limbs. His features were both rugged and kind, especially when he smiled.

I slipped out of the cave to keep watch. The young man slept only about a half hour before crawling out of the cave. Again he made gestures to show that he was grateful to me.

We communicated primarily by gestures at first. Soon my new servant showed himself much better at learning my language than I was at learning his. I called him Friday, for it was on a Friday that I rescued him. He quickly learned "yes" and "no" and the names for various items.

We spent a full day at the cave, then returned to the beach to see if his captors remained. They had gone without searching for either Friday or his pursuers.

Over time, Friday came to tell me that these trips to the island signaled victories against enemy tribes. When two tribes went to war, the victor always took the bravest enemy warriors captive. They were carried away and eaten to bring those traits of ferocity and courage to the victor. It sounded more than a little nauseating to me, but Friday felt it was natural as breathing.

When we returned to my fortress, I outfitted Friday in linen drawers and a goatskin vest. I topped this with a little rabbit-fur hat. Friday wore the clothes to please me, even though he was comfortable going about naked.

At first I lodged Friday well separate from me in a room that I could secure. But it soon became clear that was unnecessary. Never had any king a more loyal and sincere subject than Friday. He seemed almost to consider me like a father.

I found Friday eager to help in any way. He was so merry that we frequently ended laughing. Indeed, if it weren't for my fears about the return of savages, I would have been totally content on my island.

It took Friday some time to grow used to the idea of hunting with a gun. Each time I fired, he reacted with fear. I even saw him checking his own body to be certain I was not trying to shoot and kill him.

For the next three years, I taught Friday how to use of all my tools. I took him to see everything I had made. Friday was quick to help with the farming and the care of the flocks.

One day, I showed Friday the ruin of the wrecked ship. I explained that I had come upon the island the same way. That was when Friday told me the most amazing thing. He had seen such a wreck before, not far from his home.

"We save the white mans from drown," he said.

Stunned, I asked him how many men they had saved and he showed me on his fingers—seventeen.

"What happened to them?" I asked.

"They live at my nation," he said.

I had already learned that it was Friday's people who visited the west side of the island. They were much better warriors than the tribe who visited my side.

"Why did your people not kill them and eat them?" I asked.

Friday shook his head as if I were greatly confused. "We only kill when we make war fight," he explained. "We rescue the white mans. We not make war fight with them."

I was stunned at the idea of a group of Europeans so close. I took Friday to the highest point of the island where glimpses of other lands could be seen. He began jumping and dancing.

"See my country. There my nation," he said.

He seemed so overjoyed with the sight of his own country that I felt a pang. I had thought Friday happy to be with me, but perhaps my island had become a kind of captivity for him.

Captives

I told Friday that we must make him a boat at once so that he could return to his people. He looked suddenly very grave.

"Why you angry mad with Friday?" he asked.

I told him I was not angry with him at all. I only wanted him to be back to his home and his people.

"Don't you wish to be home?" I asked.

"Yes, yes," he said. "I wish we both there. No wish Friday there without you."

"What would I do there?" I asked.

"You teach," he said. "You teach Friday."

I shook my head. "You should go home and leave me alone as I was before."

"No," Friday insisted. "You save Friday. You no want Friday, you kill Friday."

At this I realized how seriously Friday took his duty to me. I urged him no more to leave, but we began work on a boat big enough to carry both of us to Friday's homeland.

I found Friday to be both a skilled worker and an able sailor. We had a tidy craft and plenty of practice. We planned to leave after the rainy season.

Right at the end of the rainy season, we awoke to learn Friday's enemies had returned. When I saw Friday's fear, I decided that this time we would not hide. With guns against their arrows, I was certain they would soon lose interest in the fight.

So we headed toward the beach to scout out the situation. A man lay upon the beach, his hands and feet tied. He was a European and had clothes on. Now it was not only Friday's countrymen for whom I fought, but my own.

Friday and I opened fire on the captors. Friday proved the better shot. We shot many and wounded still more before taking up our muskets and running to the beach.

I raced to the European, and Friday followed. He fired upon anyone who stood too close. I cut the ties that bound the man and asked him in Portuguese, "What are you?"

He responded in a whisper of Latin, "Christianus."

I asked what country he was from.

"Espaniole," he said.

I gave him a piece of bread and a drink. Then I handed him a pistol and sword for his defense. Either the bite of food or the weapons rallied him. He flew upon his captors like a fury. The enemy was in a complete panic from the gunshots and offered little resistance.

Though weakened from his time as a prisoner, the Spaniard still managed to bring down three of his captors. In the end, the beach was littered with bodies. We spotted four running for a canoe, though one was clearly wounded.

They paddled hard away from the island. Friday made two or three more shots at them but still they paddled on.

"We take boat," Friday called to me. "Not let them go."

I was concerned that they might return with their tribe and overwhelm us, so I agreed. I ran to the canoe and jumped in. Someone was already there! Another captive lay bound hand and foot.

I immediately cut his bindings and called for Friday to come and comfort the man. I gave him a small sip from my bottle and the man revived enough to sit up.

Friday took one look at the man's face and began whooping with joy. He hugged him and kissed him. Then he laughed, cried, and jumped around like a mad creature.

Finally Friday calmed enough to tell me this was his father. He rubbed his father's swollen wrists and ankles. I turned my attention to the Spaniard. Both captives were too weak to make the long walk back to my fortress. I suggested Friday paddle the canoe up the creek with both men.

To my amazement, Friday carried the Spaniard and put him gently into the canoe beside Friday's father. Then Friday paddled faster than I could walk upon the shore.

Once he reached the spot closest to my settlement, he left the men in the boat and raced back through the woods. As he passed me he said, "Go fetch more boat."

This he accomplished so quickly that he had both boats at the landing spot in the time it took me to reach there. He lifted the men gently out of the boats but there we were stopped.

Though Friday was amazingly strong, he was growing tired. He could not possibly carry two men to the fortress. Together we fashioned a kind of stretcher to lay the men on and carry them between us.

Still when we reached the outside wall of my settlement, we could go no farther. We could not carry them in and they were in no condition to climb ladders.

We built them a tent right against the wall and covered it with old sails. We made them beds of rice straw and blankets and there they recovered.

The English Ship

As we ate our first dinner, I marveled that my kingdom was populated suddenly with such a range of peoples. Friday was a Protestant, his father was a Pagan, and the Spaniard was a Papist. I thought this a fine beginning for any country.

Friday acted as interpreter both for his father and the Spaniard. I asked Friday's father what he believed the natives would do when they heard the tale from the four in the canoe.

"They not make it home," he said by way of Friday. "Very bad storm now. Bad time on sea."

I nodded for I knew the might of the sea. "But if they do make it back," I said, "will they bring others here?"

Friday's father shook his head. With the fire and roar of the guns, they were likely to think we could call down lightning. This would make this island cursed. In fact, none of that tribe ever came again to the island.

As they recovered, my new friends quickly joined in the work of the island. I found it pleasant to have so much company. But, my mind turned again to the possibility of leaving.

I asked the Spaniard if he thought the other Europeans would join us on my island. Then we could build a craft suitable for real escape. The Spaniard felt they would be most enthusiastic about the idea.

"I would not bring them now," he cautioned. "So many men here will mean food rationing. They may rebel if they are not fed."

I found his concern logical and we set about two tasks at once. We doubled the area of my plantings and planted every bit of barley and rice I could spare. We also caught more wild goats.

Then, we started boat making. We built a boat that was big enough to carry the Europeans back to my island. It was also small enough that the Spaniard and Friday's father could handle it alone.

As we worked, I was impressed at how much more quickly every task was accomplished with four men. In less than a year, the men were ready to make their voyage.

I sent them with a musket each and enough powder and shot for eight firings. They left with a good wind in October of my twenty-eighth year on the island. I was happy that my days of captivity might be nearing an end.

Some eight days after they had left, Friday called to me one morning, "They are come. They are come."

I jumped up and turned my glass to the sea. The boat I saw was not of our making. I recognized it as an English ship. And the boat drawing ever nearer shore was an English longboat.

You might think I would rush the shore in great joy, but something made me uneasy. What was an English ship doing here?

Friday and I slipped quietly through the jungle to get a clearer vision of the shore. The longboat drew close. I counted eleven men aboard, though three of them were bound.

When the boat reached shore, the free men hauled the bound men out upon the shore. It was clear that the bound men feared for their lives.

"The English men eat prisoners," Friday whispered as we through the trees. "They will eat them."

"No, no," I said. "I believe they will murder them. But they will not eat them."

I wished now that Friday's father and the Spaniard were here to help. I watched closely as two of the men stayed with the longboat. The three prisoners sat in a miserable huddle. The rest of the group wandered into the brush.

I crept close and peered into the boat. The two men there had fallen asleep. So I slipped back behind the prisoners and cut their bindings. I stood and asked, "What are ye, gentlemen?"

The men stared at me openmouthed but gave no answer.

"Gentlemen, do not be surprised at me," I said. "Perhaps you have a friend where you least expected."

The poor man began to weep as he said, "Are you a real man or an angel?"

"If I were an angel," I said with a smile, "I am certain I would be better dressed."

The man calmed slightly at my lack of fear. He told me he was the captain of the ship I had spied. A small group of evil men had led the crew to mutiny. Two of these villains were ashore now.

I could certainly wait until the men left and simply let the captain and his men join my kingdom. But, I was not inclined to lose the opportunity to leave the island.

"If I help you," I said, "will you accept my command while on my island? And will you take me with you when you leave?"

The captain assured me with great enthusiasm. So I gave each a musket.

"I believe," the captain said, "that if we kill the two leaders of this group, the others will lose their taste for mutiny."

I found the idea of such killing distasteful. The captain assured me that if we let the men live, they would only die later by hanging. There was no other future for them in England.

At that, we went in search of the men. We found them settled down to sleep not far away. One of the men heard us coming. He called out to the others, who jumped up.

The captain fired upon the leaders of the group. The blast killed one and wounded the other, who ran at the captain. The captain struck him with the butt of his musket and the man fell down to rise no more.

The other men swore their loyalty to the captain quickly enough. We divided our captives into groups and settled some in the cave. The rest were housed in the fortress.

I told the captain the story of my time on the island. He was amazed at all I had been through. Talk turned then to how we might secure the captain's ship.

"Soon they will surely send another boat to check on their missing crewmen, don't you agree?" I asked.

The captain agreed. We decided our first task must be to make the longboat unusable. Then, they could not simply take it and leave the missing men to their fate.

We returned to the longboat and gathered the food stored in it. There was a great lump of sugar and a few biscuit cakes, which were a treat after so long eating island food.

We bashed a hole in the longboat so it would not float. But, the hole was not so large that it could not be repaired if we wished. We buried the mutineers that had died. Then we waited.

Soon enough, another boat was launched. The captain used my glass to check each man.

He said that three of the men had joined the mutiny by force and should be spared. The rest were all villains.

"Then they shall live or die as they behave toward us," I said.

We waited on shore, assuming they would bring the boat entirely to the sand as they had before. Instead, the longboat let off a group of men and rowed back to anchor.

This made our situation tricky. If we attacked the men, the boat offshore would eventually simply leave. We had to bring it ashore.

We watched as the men on the beach examined the broken boat and called out for their missing men. Finally they gave up and signaled for the longboat to collect them. Then I had an idea.

I sent Friday and the mate to call to the men on the beach just as the longboat landed. They were to lead them on a merry tour of the jungle, staying out of sight the whole way. They immediately put this into practice.

At the sound of shouts, the leader of the group commanded the two men in the longboat to wait on shore. As soon as the group disappeared, we quickly captured the men in the boat. One was knocked down into the sand with the butt of the gun. The other yielded without a fight and offered to join us immediately.

We waited several hours until Friday and the mate rejoined us. We heard the weary sounds of the men returning soon after.

CHAPTER 17

Securing the Ship

The wandering men were confused to find the longboat empty. They peered into the darkness, clearly frightened.

The captain rushed out of hiding and began shooting. The boatswain, whom the captain had declared the most evil of them all, fell on the spot.

The mutineers were in a panic, for they could not make out our numbers in the darkness. I told the man we had captured to call to them.

"Tom Smith!" the man shouted. "Tom Smith!"

"Who's that?" Tom Smith answered. "Is that you, Robinson?"

As the man we had captured was Robinson, he answered, "Aye, throw down your arms and yield. There are too many of them to fight."

"How many?" Tom Smith yelled. "And who are they?"

"The governor of the island has captured us with a troupe of fifty men," Robinson said. "Will Frye is wounded and I am prisoner."

"If we yield," Tom Smith said, "will they not kill us?"

"I will ask the captain," Robinson said. "The governor has talked with him."

"All will be safe if you lay down your arms!" the captain shouted.

At this, they all laid down their arms and begged for their lives. Those the captain said were not trustworthy were bound. Then we set to a plan to recapture the ship.

I had the captain talk to the men one by one and bring with us only those he trusted with his life. We gathered twelve men that the captain felt confident in. This group would recapture the ship.

Friday and I would remain on shore since our appearance would be recognized as not part of the crew. We would watch over the remaining captives.

We swiftly repaired the damaged longboat and launched both to return to the ship after darkness had fallen. As soon as they came near the ship, Robinson called out. No one aboard the ship seemed at all nervous of the approaching longboats.

When the captain and the mate gained the ship, a swift battle began and ended. Most of the crew laid down arms quickly. Only the new rebel captain, two of his men, and the ship's cabin boy fled to the roundhouse.

The captain ordered the door to the roundhouse broken open. As soon as the door burst in, the rebel captain fired and wounded the mate.

Though wounded, the mate rushed into the roundhouse and shot the rebel captain. The others yielded without further fight.

As soon as the ship was secured, the captain ordered the firing of seven guns, which was a signal to me that the ship was secure. When I heard the signal, I lay down to rest.

I was awakened the next day by a voice crying, "Governor!" The captain climbed the hill to stand before me, grinning and pointing to the ship.

"My dear friend," he said, "there's your ship. You saved her."

I looked out at the ship that rode within a half mile of shore. The reality that I could now leave the island overwhelmed me, and I nearly fainted.

The captain presented me with lavish gifts for my help, including a suit of clothes from his own things. I found them disagreeable to wear, but I welcomed the return to civilization that they represented.

The captain and I discussed what to do with the remaining prisoners. As mutineers, they would be hanged if returned to England. I offered the men the chance to stay on the island.

I made them swear to welcome the Spaniards and work together with them. I spent some time showing them the work and resources of the island.

The men agreed, though two eventually begged us to take them away, even if it meant their deaths. The captain allowed them to rejoin the crew after a lesser punishment.

Thus, Friday and I left our island in the hands of three Englishmen. I knew the island would treat them well if they were wise.

On December 19, 1687, I left the island where I had lived twenty-eight years, two months, and nineteen days.

Strange Homeland

In June, we arrived in England. I was a perfect stranger in my homeland. My parents were both dead. The only family I found were my two sisters, one widowed and one poorly married.

I met with the widow of my friend and found her in poverty but still as good and honest as ever. I gave her all I could spare.

I found a ship to carry me to Lisbon, where I hoped to learn the fate of my plantation in the Brazils. I searched for the kindhearted Portuguese captain. His knowledge of the state of my plantation was sketchy, but he said he believed it was doing well. He offered to help me get it back.

In time, my plantation was set back in my name, and I learned how much my fortune had grown. I was now wealthy beyond anything I could have hoped.

I immediately sent a gift to each of my sisters and to the widow of my old friend. I hoped that they might have more ease in their lives.

I decided to return to England. But, I found myself uncomfortable setting foot again on a ship. Though I approached three different ships, even going so far as moving my things aboard, I pulled back from each before sailing.

I do not think it was superstition that kept me on land but the nudging of God. Indeed two of the ships I had considered boarding experienced hard fates—one falling to pirates and another shipwrecked with only three survivors.

So I planned a journey by land. Friday and I picked up one young Englishman, two English merchants, and two young Portuguese gentlemen by the time of our leaving. Add to that five servants and we had quite a group for the road.

We traveled comfortably enough until we reached ten days out from Old Castile. The weather turned from hot to bitter cold.

Friday was positively terrified at the sight of the snow-covered mountain, for he had never known snow or cold. After years in the tropics, I also found the cold difficult to bear.

We arrived in Pampeluna in a blizzard. We could take no step without fear of being buried alive in the drifted snow. We stayed twenty days in Pampeluna, until four French gentlemen arrived safely with a guide.

We sent for this guide and he agreed to lead us. "You will need to be well armed," he warned. "With this early winter, you may see wolves driven by hunger."

"We have no fear of those," I said. "Though I have heard of two-legged wolves which sometimes attack travelers on the French side of the mountains."

The guide assured us that his route would keep us well away from such dangers. We set out with our guide on November 15. We began by doubling back on the road we had already passed so we might attempt the mountains from another direction.

In the mountains, we found the way far less snowy and dangerous, though we were stopped upon the trail for two days because of snow. This worried us, but the guide promised it would soon pass.

That evening, about two hours before dark, our guide rode just ahead and out of sight. Suddenly, wolves bolted out of a hollow in front of him. Two of them attacked the guide. One snapped and bit at the horse and the other leaped to attack the man directly.

"Help!" the guide shouted as the wolf tried to pull him from the saddle.

At the guide's panicky call, Friday pulled out his pistol and rushed ahead of us. When he saw the attack upon the guide, he shouted, "Master!" Then he shot the wolf.

The other wolf fled when his companion fell to the ground. At the boom of Friday's pistol, the most dismal sound of howling rose around us.

The guide's horse seemed uninjured, but the same could not be said for the guide. The wolf had bitten him twice, once in the arm and once in the leg.

Friday was helping the man from his horse when the rest of us caught up with them. We took in both the guide's wounds and something Friday had not yet seen. A great bear was trudging out of the trees toward my friend.

Now a bear normally wants no contact with a man. But in the bitter starvation of an early winter, any animal can turn vicious with hunger. While anyone else would consider the approach of a bear frightening, Friday only grinned and said, "I show him some trick."

He dashed up the road past the bear, popping the bear in the head with a stone as he passed. The bear ran after Friday at a gallop. Friday set down his gun before scrambling up a great oak tree beside the road.

The bear sniffed the gun as he passed it, but left it alone. It scrambled up the tree after Friday. Friday kept easily ahead, finally choosing a high branch to walk out on. The bear crept out on the branch after my friend.

The bear's great bulk made the branch sway. The beast froze. Then Friday jumped on the branch, making it bounce. The bear cast a panicked glance around him, for they were high in the tree.

The bear could neither back up nor go forward because of his shaky position. Friday crept out to the end of the branch, making it bend until it nearly touched the branch below it. My friend used these bent branches to slip quickly from the tree.

"Now I'll shoot the bear," I yelled.

"No!" Friday called back. "No shoot if him no more want fight."

The bear edged slowly backward out of the tree. Friday stood at the bottom of the tree with his pistol in hand.

When the bear reached the ground, he turned his head to roar into Friday's face. Then, my friend shot him dead.

New Adventures

Normally I would have skinned the bear and the wolf and taken the hides. But the guide needed attention and we were still long upon the trail. We patched the guide's wounds and pressed on, leaving the creatures where they lay.

"Are we in danger still from the wolves?" I asked the guide.

He nodded and urged us to keep our weapons at the ready. At one point we spotted five wolves crossing the road ahead, but they took no notice of us.

When darkness had fully fallen, we came upon the carcass of a horse. A pack of at least a dozen wolves tore at what little remained of it. We eased past them and continued on while the wolves stayed on the carcass.

We had not gone far when we spotted a great rush of wolves coming at us. It seemed hundreds in the darkness. We fired into the groups to scatter them. We shouted and bellowed. The wolves shied but did not go away.

Then, we heard more gunshots just up ahead and we looked in surprise at one another. Were we not the only travelers that night? Then at another opening in the wood, a saddled horse leaped out onto the road with a full pack of wolves flying after him.

We rushed to the break in the woods and found the carcass of another horse and two men besides. Near one man lay a gun, probably the same we had heard shot. Both the men and the horse were already much eaten.

Near this spot were some large timber trees that had been cut down. I called my little troop to line up with one of the fallen trees in front of us. The wolves made a furious charge at us, growling and panting.

We fired in a pattern of every other man in the row so that while one group was firing, another was reloading. We felled dozens of wolves and yet they seemed to keep coming.

I feared the wolves would outlast our powder, so I used some to create a small fuse to the pile of dry trees. I snapped a spark close to the powder. The blaze did more to push back the wolves than any of our shooting.

A few of the wolves had the courage to approach the fire and we quickly dispatched them. The remaining turned tail and ran.

We pressed forward again upon the trail. We heard wolves howl in the wood and caught sight of their shadowy passing. But no more came out to fight with us.

We finally reached the town where we were to lodge. The villagers told us they kept a guard night and day because of the hunger of the bears and the wolves.

In the morning, it was clear our guide's arm and leg were badly infected. We hired a new guide from the town and pressed on. We were soon out of the snow and reached Dover by January.

⊰C∼⊱

After such an adventure, I decided I would rather travel by sea in storm and pirate than to ever try to cross those mountains again.

I stayed awhile with the dear widow of my old friend and decided to sell my plantation. I wrote to the kind, retired Portuguese captain and he handled the sale for me. I now had a sizable fortune.

I longed to see my island again and find out how the Spaniards had fared with the mutineers. When I mentioned it to the old widow, she was so horrified that I put the idea away for a time.

I took the two sons of my brother into my care. The eldest became quite a gentleman. Since he was bold and enterprising, I put him on a good ship and sent him to sea.

I married and had three children, two sons and one daughter. Then my wife died. When my nephew returned from a successful voyage to Spain, he engaged me as a private trader to the East Indies. I took the offer eagerly.

In 1694, I revisited my island and found a growing colony. The Spaniards had trouble with the villains I had left behind, but they handled it well.

The Spaniards had improved the island and taken wives from the tribes on the other islands. I found at least twenty children in the colony.

I stayed there twenty days and left them with a wealth of fresh supplies. I promised the men I would go and seek more wives who might enjoy the adventure of the colony.

Though I left the island, I did not abandon adventure. Indeed, I entered into another ten years of such excitement. I might even tell you of it, someday.